MW00877927

The Good Witch of Salem

written by

Ashley Tina

illustrated by

Zuzana Svobodová

The Good Witch of Salem

Copyright © 2020 by Ashley Tina

All rights reserved. No part of this publication may be reproduced, distributed, stored in a retrieval system, or transmitted in any form or by any means, including electronic, photocopying, recording or mechanical methods without prior written permission from Ashley Tina, except in the case of brief quotations embodied in critical reviews.

For all permission requests, please write to:
ashleytina@goodwitchofsalem.com

ISBN: 978-1-73523-181-5 (hardcover)
ISBN: 978-1-73523-180-8 (paperback)
ISBN: 978-1-73523-182-2 (eBook)

Library of Congress Control Number:

Illustrations by Zuzana Svobodová
Book Design by Zuzana Svobodová

Discover the magic at www.goodwitchofsalem.com

To my parents who have taught
me that the impossible is so
beautifully possible...

I am Magical

My kind heart travels
wherever I go.
Good deeds
always follow.
Just watch and
I'll show.

Salem is my home where
I glimmer and shine,
helping and healing others
with all my potions in mind.
Aura, my cat, is my helper indeed.
She always can sense
when someone is in need.
In need of love, hope,
or a little bit of joy.
Anything to help
a little girl or boy.

Here in our home or on adventures we seek,
Aura shines colors and I do take a peek.
I see purple, green, pink, and some gray.
They each have a magical meaning to convey.

"Oh Aura!" I gasp. "I can feel it too.

Helping and healing is what we are meant to do.

There's someone in need of love in the purest kind.

Let's take a closer look to see what we find."

My crystal ball,
where could it be?
I look on my shelves
and all around,
but nothing
can be found.

I look over past Aura
and I can see,
it's out catching

the full

moon's

energy!

"Thank you, Aura!" I say with glee.

Now I can look within and see.

I place my crystal ball

within my two calm hands.

The room grows quiet

and dim as it commands.

I stop. I breathe.
I clear my mind.

I make myself open for
what I am meant to find.

"Angels protect me
as I seek what's in need.
White light surround me
as I take the lead."

The crystal beams and fills the room with light.
This is how I know everything is just right.
I go within and begin to see
the symbols and images that come to me.

A bouquet of balloons appear
as children run around without a care.
The sweet smell of cupcakes fill the air,
and laughter is all I can hear.
The screeches of glee make
me feel joyous and free.

The happiness
takes over me.

I keep searching for more to be found.

I wait. I focus. I look around.

Pop! Goes a balloon. The laughter it breaks.

That's when I feel quite an ache.

There is no more music or bright, shiny light.
The candles go out and so does my sight.
Things start to get foggy, misty, and gray.
I have the feeling that no one is left to play.

It is sad.   It is lonely.   I feel such hurt.

The laughter is gone and so is the dessert.

The session it ends and there is no more left to see.

I clear my crystal ball from its energy.

Just then my broom meets my hand

as I dance and I sweep to clear the space and the land.

"To find true joy we must start from within.

A glitz and a glitter, now let's begin!"

We create magic that heals through colors that shine.

Each one has its own meaning to define.

Rose quartz is pink for hope, belief, and a cure.

There is never enough pink, so let's add some more!

Amethyst purple is to heal and create.

The peace deep inside will help you see your true fate.

Sapphire blue from the sea and the sky

gives everlasting ease, you might want to try.

Yellow topaz shines bright with sparkles galore.

It's used to bring inner happiness for one to explore.

Citrine orange uplifts and brings upon new friends

with love and some laughter that transcends.

Emerald green offers growth and vitality

for balance that's in perfect harmony.

Ruby red sparkles to give healing energy.

Its power will help you to truly be free.

Each color it glows, it sparkles, it shines!

Gleaming from my cauldron to deliver some kind.

We mix and we mash. Then we drop and we stir.

A glitter.

A glitz.

But wait, there is more!

The colors are poured into a miraculous mold.

To create a heart that's worth more than gold.

The colors in the heart

will heal right from the start.

Purple, green, yellow, orange, red, pink and blue.

Nothing could ever be so true.

We must go find this girl who needs

kindness **and** love.

Our guides will lead us from up above.

Aura and I look all over town,
then I spot a familiar face
wearing a frown.

"Hello, how are you?

Are you hurt? Are you sad?

What can I do to erase all the mad?

I saw you were happy, and then it did end.

You appeared to be in need of

a very good friend."

For just a moment, I thought she was going to depart.

Then she looks up with some hope in *her heart.*

"Yes, you are right. I am sad. I am hurt.
I feel lost and alone like I was left in the dirt.

My happiness did end and I wish it was still here.
It's really hard to find it, through all this foggy air.

I can't find my own way.
I don't even want to go out to play.
There's nothing left for me to say."

"The place you must start is within your own heart.
From there, you will heal, once you can feel
everything inside you that's real.

Kindness and love is deep within you.
Find it, use it, and you'll be truer than true.
Be your best self, but most of all just be you.

My cat Aura and I mixed up

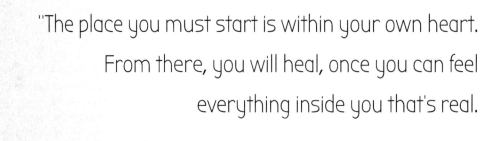

a rainbow potion

to help you balance all
of the commotion."

"This heart is a healing amulet for you to wear.

It will heal any sadness, discomfort, or regret you may bare.

Each color represents amazing parts of your life.

They will glow and shine you away from strife."

"Find your passion and don't let it go.
Do what you love and from there you will grow.
Share kindness with others and help those in need.
Always live your life fully and you will succeed."

"Thank you, Good Witch of Salem. I will do that indeed.
I am grateful for all the love you have shown me."

"Now get on your way and do not lose any hope.
You have everything you need
and more to cope."

The sun it sets and the day is done.

I did some good healing and had a little fun.

It's time to rest before more kindness can be done.

Aura and I hope you will join us again for magical fun.

We have only just begun.

Ashley Tina is an Elementary School Teacher and Creative Entrepreneur. Teaching a diversity of young minds for over ten years led Ashley to see the need to develop kindness and amplify the lessons in the classroom to wider audiences of all ages. Yoga, nature, and art are just a few of her many passions in life. Ashley resides North of Boston with her husband and two little Good Witches.

Zuzana Svobodová is an illustrator. Her love of drawing began from the time she could grab a pencil. She still loves children's books and can spend hours in bookstores looking at illustrations and discovering new stories. She enjoys yoga, reading with her kids and baking sweets.